This book is dedicated the star of the
story and the little boy who stole my
heart from the instant he was born.
For Max

It was a warm spring day.
The birds were chirping,
the flowers were blooming
the sun was shining and
Max wasn't enjoying
any of it as he was
fast asleep in
his comfy bed.

'Max' shouted mum from
downstairs 'are you ever
going to get up? You do
realise what day
it is don't you?'

IT'S MY BIRTHDAY. WHERE'S MY PRESENTS?

'Now Max. That's not how we start off our day is it? Even if it is your birthday!' 'Sorry Mum' said Max getting his breath back. Good morning Mum, good morning Dad, good morning sis!!'

'Good morning my darling' said Mum
'Morning pal' said dad as he wiped peanut butter
off his t-shirt (it had dripped off his toast!)
Izzy (Max's older sister) looked over at him, looked him up
and down, shook her head and went back to
playing on her phone.

Max sat down to eat his cereal for breakfast and as he slurped the milk off his spoon, he eyed a small pile of presents on the other side of the kitchen table.

After he had finished his cereal Mum said. 'Now Max, we know you are very excited about your birthday. You know Gran and Granddad are coming over later for a tea party and for you to open your presents, but Dad and I have had a chat and you may open one this morning!'

On the table were 3 presents. Tightly wrapped. Max studied
them closely. He could see one of them was round in shape
'clearly a football!' Thought Max (Max loved football you see).
The next one was almost completely flat and flopped about
when he shook it 'clearly a football kit!' Thought Max
(Max loved football you see)

The third one he couldn't work out. It was a rectangular box.
Max picked it up. 'Too heavy to be a book' he thought. He shook it.
There weren't any noises to give away what it could be.

'Mum. I'm going to open this one!' He said tearing off the football wrapping paper (Max loved football you see)

When the paper was all over the floor Max looked at his new present WOW he gasped. It was the new MiScreen Pro (with a watch) tablet. The MiScreen pro could do EVERYTHING! you could call, you could text, you could video call, you could app, double app, triple app... you name it. The MiScreen pro could do it

Max burst into his bedroom and leapt into his bed. He fumbled with the box and ripped off the lid.

There it was. New and sleek and shiny. Max took it out of the box and turned it on. Whilst he was waiting he - strapped the watch to his wrist. The black screen came to life and the words 'MiScreen. Taking you anywhere you want to go' appeared on the screen.

WAHHHHHHHH. THANK YOU MUM, THANK YOU DAD, THANK YOU IZZY!'

When the words disappeared and the home screen popped up. Max expected to see lots of apps ready to be pressed. Instead there was just one app. It was green and looked like a football pitch. Max pressed the app and without warning, there was a loud "WHOOSH" and Max was sucked straight into the football pitch shaped app.

Max had never moved so fast in his life!
He zipped through a brightly coloured tunnel.
Twisting, turning, floating and falling
until "THWACK" he landed hard on his bottom.

Max had landed somewhere very big and very noisy. He shook his head and looked around. Max could see bright lights, hear loud singing and cheering. He had landed in football stadium — he had landed on the substitutes bench in a football stadium! Max couldn't believe what he was seeing. Suddenly he heard a loud voice saying "Max, get w armed up, we need you to try and help us win the game!" Max looked down. To his surprise he was wearing a bright red football jersey with white shorts and black socks.

Next thing Max knew he was standing on the halfway line. He could see the score was 1-1. He high fived the tired looking player coming off and ran to take his position in attack.

The ball was being pinged and zipped around the green grass at a lightning speed. The ball got played out wide and the fast running winger chased it and whipped in a high cross. The striker and defender leapt for the ball, the defender was taller so he headed it high into the air.

Max watched the ball
rise into the air.
It seemed to stop in mid
air before starting to fall.
Max ran toward the ball,
never taking his eyes off it,
he brought back his right foot
and swung it forward just
as the ball dropped in
front of him.

He felt his boot hit the ball and there was a hush from the crowd.
He didn't dare look up in case he had kicked the ball way over the top of the bar.

Suddenly, and surprisingly there was a huge ROAR in the stadium. Max looked up just as the ball tore into the top corner of the net. The crowd had gone wild, the players on his team had gone wild. Somewhere in the chaos he heard the referee blow the final whistle. Max had won the game with the last kick of the game!

He waited for the THWACK of his bottom hitting something hard, but thankfully this time he landed on something soft.

He looked around and quickly realized he'd landed on his bed.
He could hear his Mum calling him to open the rest of his presents as his grandparents were in the kitchen.

'Wow. What an adventure!!' he thought as he looked at his MiScreen.
I wonder where I'll go on my next one.

As Max ran downstairs to open the rest of his presents, his MiScreen was busy
downloading new apps. These apps had pictures of dinosaurs, pirates, UFOs,
lost treasure and lots more. So, Max. The answer to where you're
going to go on your next adventure is entirely up to you!

The End

THE CORNER BARBERS

CALL:
07712022261

66 HIGH STREET
GLYNNEATH
SA11 5DA

static caravan holidays

www.static-caravan-hire.co.uk

C.A.HAWKES

Painting & Decorating Services

07399924031
cahawkespainting@gmail.com

A1 GARDEN SOLUTIONS

07577952170

WATERS ROOFING

Call on:
01639 676557

OnSite

0345 6006374

www.onsite.co.uk

First Financial Wales

☎ 01 639 262 222

✉ Lynsey@ffswales.co.uk

Securing the present - Protecting your future

BE RULED CLOTHING

📱 07 931 254 571

R&E Heating Ltd

CALL: 07539057284

01639419102

HOUSE OF GLAM

Hair and beauty salon
TONNA

01 639 637 999

Printed in Great Britain
by Amazon